SAY HELLO TO ZORRO!

CARTER GOODRICH

SIMON & SCHUSTER BOOKS FOR YOUNG READERS

New York   London   Toronto   Sydney

FOR LANEY, WHO HAS TO DEAL WITH JULES AND MAGGIE'S SCHEDULE

SIMON & SCHUSTER BOOKS FOR YOUNG READERS • An imprint of Simon & Schuster Children's Publishing Division • 1230 Avenue of the Americas, New York, New York 10020 • Copyright © 2011 by Carter Goodrich • All rights reserved, including the right of reproduction in whole or in part in any form. • SIMON & SCHUSTER BOOKS FOR YOUNG READERS is a trademark of Simon & Schuster, Inc. • For information about special discounts for bulk purchases, please contact Simon & Schuster Special Sales at 1-866-506-1949 or business@simonandschuster.com. • The Simon & Schuster Speakers Bureau can bring authors to your live event. For more information or to book an event, contact the Simon & Schuster Speakers Bureau at 1-866-248-3049 or visit our website at www.simonspeakers.com. • Book design by Dan Potash • The text for this book is set in Gorey. • The illustrations for this book are rendered in watercolor. • Manufactured in China • 0111 SCP • 10 9 8 7 6 5 4 3 2 1 • Library of Congress Cataloging-in-Publication Data • Goodrich, Carter. • Say hello to Zorro! / Carter Goodrich.—1st ed. • p. cm • Summary: Mister Bud, the family dog, has a satisfying routine to his life, but when another dog joins the family and disrupts his schedule, Mister Bud must learn to adapt. • ISBN 978-1-4169-3894-4 (hardcover) • [1. Dogs—Fiction. 2. Change—Fiction.] I. Title. • PZ7.G6147Say 2010 • [E]—dc22 • 2009011484

MISTER BUD HAD IT PRETTY GOOD. EVERYTHING WAS JUST RIGHT.

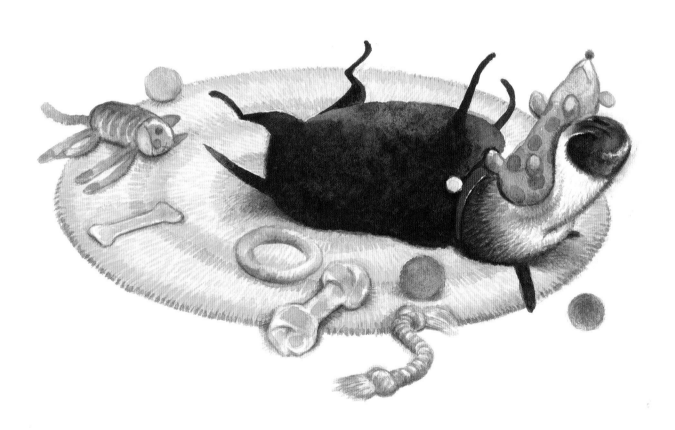

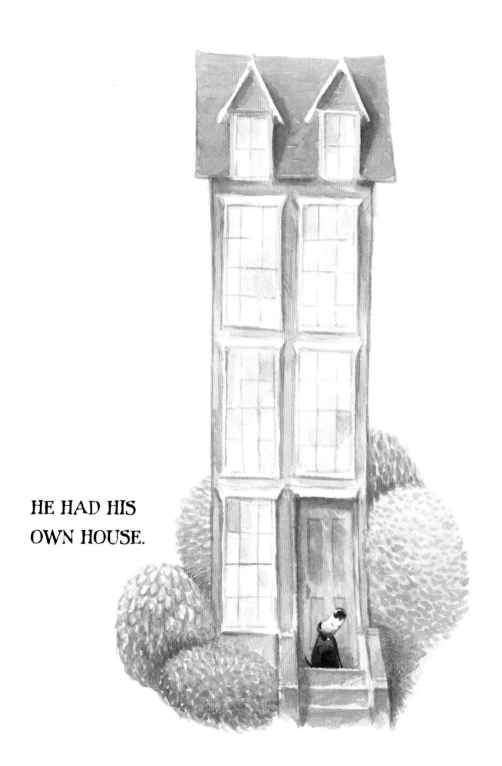

HE HAD HIS
OWN HOUSE.

HIS OWN BED.

HIS OWN TOYS.

HIS OWN DISH.

BUT MOST OF ALL . . .

HE HAD HIS OWN SCHEDULE.
AND EVERYBODY STUCK TO THE SCHEDULE.

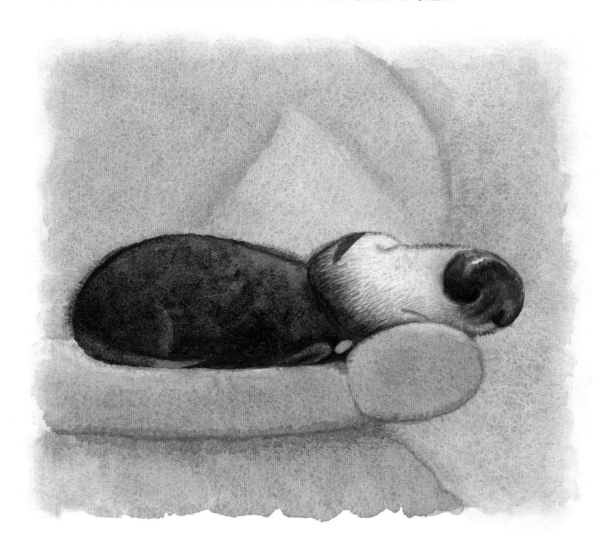

IT WENT LIKE THIS. . . .

1. WAKE-UP TIME

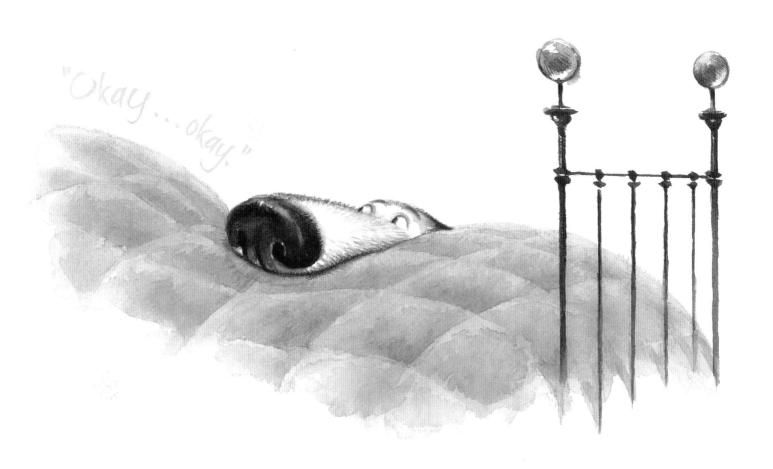

"Okay... okay."

2. BISCUIT, THEN A WALK TIME

3. NAP TIME

4. SHIFT-POSITION-AND-NAP-SOME-MORE TIME

5. WAIT AND WATCH TIME

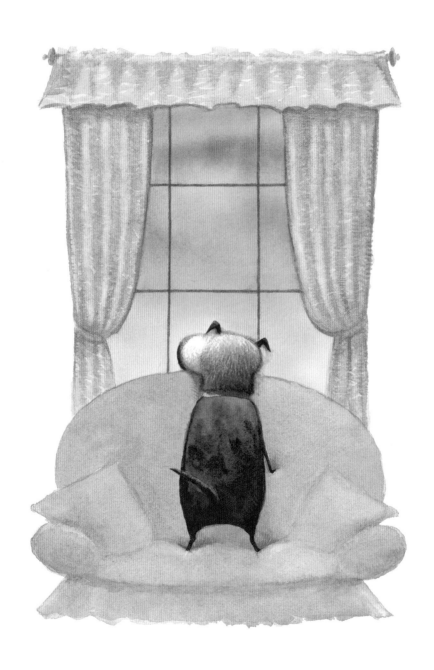

6. GREET AND MAKE A FUSS TIME

7. QUICK BACKYARD TIME

9. AFTER-DINNER WALK TIME

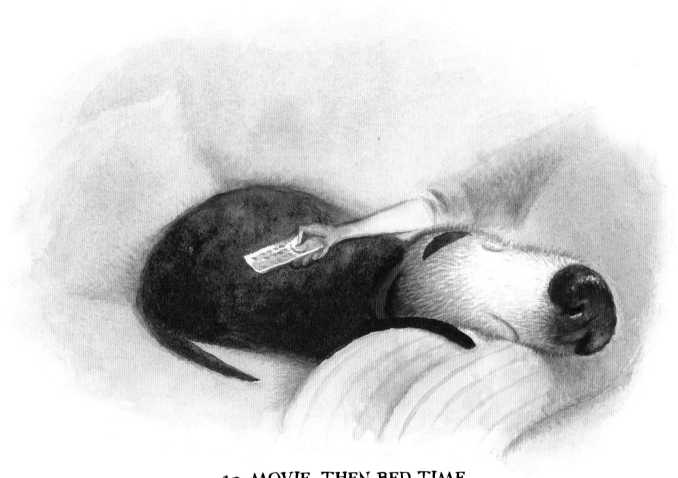

10. MOVIE, THEN BED TIME

THAT WAS IT. THAT WAS THE SCHEDULE.
AND EVERYBODY STUCK TO THE SCHEDULE.

NO EXCEPTIONS.

ONE DAY, RIGHT AT GREET AND MAKE A FUSS TIME . . .

*"Mister Bud, say hello to Zorro!
Zorro is moving in with us!"*

THERE WAS A STRANGER.

AND THERE WAS TROUBLE.

"Now, you two get along," THEY WERE TOLD.

IT WASN'T EASY AT FIRST.
ZORRO HAD HIS OWN THINGS,
AND HE COULD BE BOSSY.

BEAT IT.

MISTER BUD HAD HIS OWN THINGS,
AND HE COULD BE GRUMPY.

WHAT DO
YOU
WANT?

BUT THEN . . .

SOMETHING SURPRISING HAPPENED.

MISTER BUD AND ZORRO FOUND OUT
THEY HAD THE SAME SCHEDULE!

SUDDENLY THE WALKS WERE MORE FUN. . . .

NAP TIME WAS MORE COMFORTABLE.

GREET AND MAKE A FUSS TIME WAS MUCH LOUDER.

EVEN MOVIE, THEN BED TIME WAS MORE EXCITING.

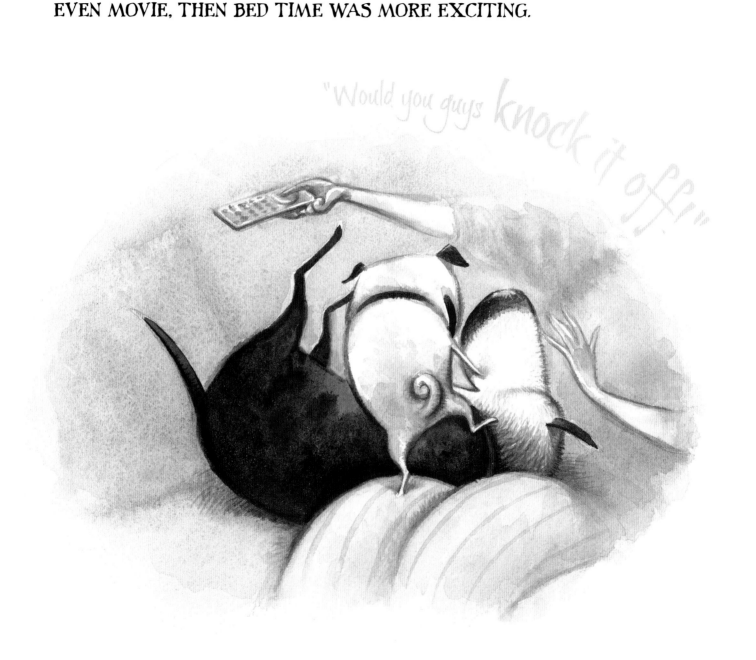

SO, EVEN THOUGH MISTER BUD
WAS STILL SOMETIMES GRUMPY,

BACK OFF, ZORRO.

AND ZORRO COULD STILL BE PRETTY BOSSY,

HEY! THAT'S MY DISH!

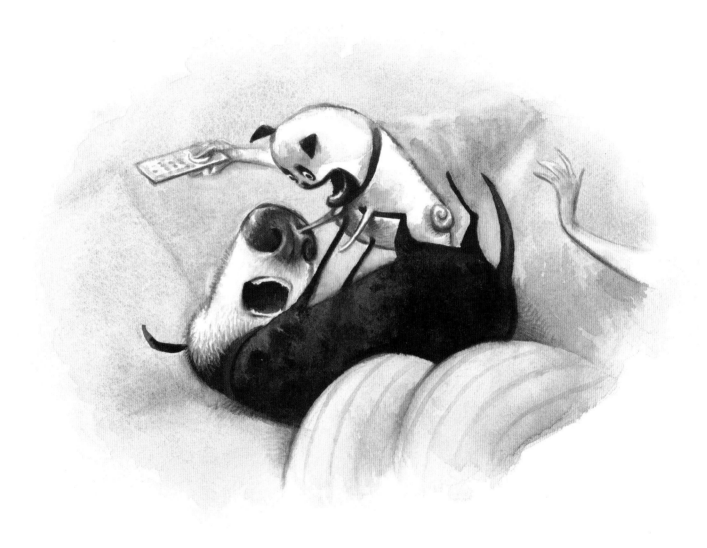

THEY BECAME BEST FRIENDS,

AND EVERYBODY STUCK TO THE SCHEDULE.